GWYNEDD-MERCY COLLEGE
GWYNEDD VALLEY PA 19437

DISCARD

P9-CQX-738

LOURDES LIBRARY
GWYNEDD MERCY COLLEGE
GWYNEDD VALLEY, PA 19437

DISCARD

PIC
KL
199
DISCARD

LOURDES LIBRARY
GWYNEDD-MERCY COLLEGE
DISCARD
GWYNEDD VALLEY, PA 19437

13.50 - 9.18

The LION and the LITTLE RED BIRD

story and pictures by

ELISA KLEVEN

DUTTON CHILDREN'S BOOKS
New York

3059

One afternoon, a little red bird
saw a lion
with a bushy green tail,
as green as the forest.
The bird had never seen anything so unusual
and so pretty.
Just looking at it made her happy.

"Lion, Lion!" she said.
"Why is your tail so green?"
The lion didn't understand the bird's language.
He thought she was simply chirping.
He smiled at her

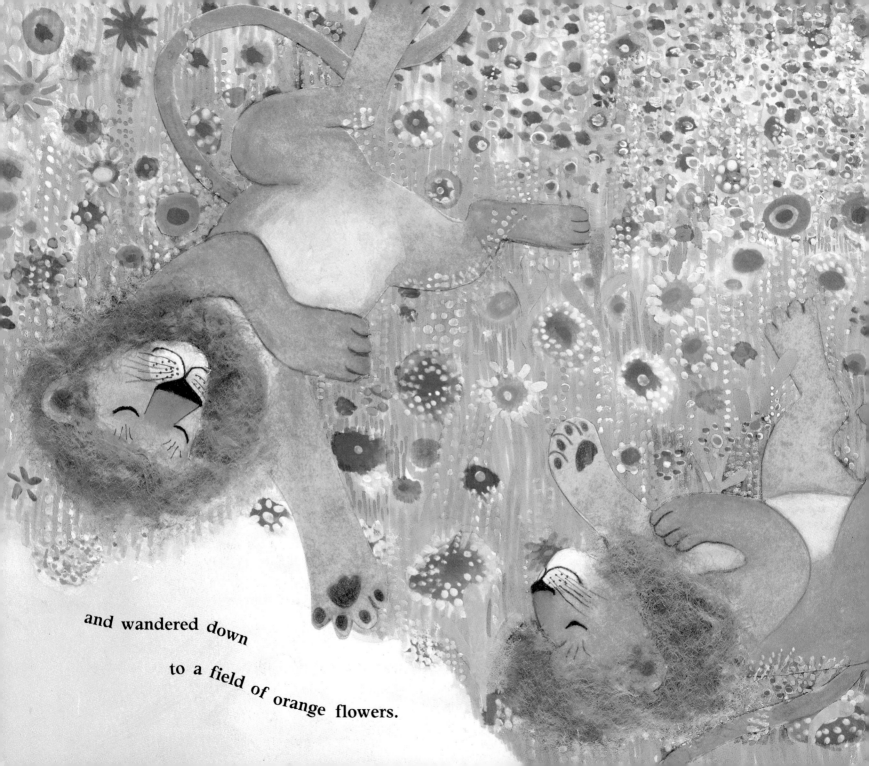

and wandered down
to a field of orange flowers.

The bird watched him roll and sniff

and chase butterflies,

then slowly walk west with the setting sun
and disappear into a cave.
The bird waited on a tree nearby.
She wanted to see the lion's green tail again.
But the lion did not come out of the cave,
so the bird made herself a soft nest
and slept through the warm starry night.

In the morning the lion came out,
swishing his tail—
which was no longer green, but orange as a flower,
orange as a butterfly,
orange as the setting sun.
"Lion, Lion!" the bird chirped, astonished.
"Why is your tail so orange?"
Again, the lion did not understand the bird.
He smiled at her

and climbed over the hill

and up the mountain

to a deep blue lake
beneath a bright blue sky,
where he soaked his tired paws
while the bird splashed nearby.

At the end of the day
the lion climbed
back down the mountain,
over the hill,

and home to his cave.
The bird settled down in the tree,
wondering, as the sky darkened,
about the lion and his orange tail.

But in the morning
the lion's tail was no longer orange.
It was blue as the brightest blue sky,
blue as the deep mountain lake where he'd soaked his paws.
"Lion, Lion!" the bird chirped, enchanted.
"How did your tail change from orange to blue?
Are you a magician?"
The lion just smiled

and ambled over to a bush
full of shiny red berries.
They were beautiful berries, but very sour.
"Lion," the bird chirped, making a face,
"these berries are still too sour to eat!
Why don't you pick them when they are ripe?"
The lion just smiled,
thinking how much he liked the bird's chirping company.

All afternoon the lion picked berries
while the bird nibbled sunflower seeds nearby.
Once, when the lion stepped on a thorn,
the bird pulled it out for him.

At sundown, the lion swished his tail good-bye
and returned to his cave.
The bird settled down in her nest.
She wondered what color the lion's tail
would be in the morning.
She wished he would answer her questions.

During the night a storm came.
Thunder crashed and lightning flashed.
Rain swept away the bird's nest.
Hearing the noise, the lion rushed out
and reached up into the tree
where the bird crouched, shivering and scared.
He lifted her down

and carried her into his cave.
The cave was warm and colorful.
The walls were filled with pictures

of green forests, orange flowers,
butterflies, sunsets,
a bright blue sky, and a deep blue lake.

"Lion, Lion!" the bird chirped, delighted.
"How did these pictures get here?"
The lion smiled,
dipped his tail into a bowl
of shiny red berry juice,
and painted a picture of the bird,
chirping on a berry bush.
The bird sang while the lion painted.
She sang a song without any questions,
full of color and joy.
The lion had never heard anything so unusual
and so pretty.
Just listening made him happy.

In the morning, the storm was past.
The world shone fresh and bright.
The lion's tail was berry-red,
and the little bird knew why.
She sang her happiest song

and wondered what
the lion would paint
that night.

for Mia

Copyright © 1992 by Elisa Kleven

All rights reserved.

Library of Congress Cataloging-in-Publication Data

Kleven, Elisa.
　The lion and the little red bird / by Elisa Kleven.—1st ed.
　　　p.　cm.
　Summary: A little bird discovers why the lion's tail changes color
each day.
　ISBN 0-525-44898-5
　[1. Color—Fiction.　2. Lions–Fiction.　3. Birds—Fiction.]
I. Title.
PZ7.K6783875Li　1992
[E]—dc20　　　91-36691　CIP　AC

Published in the United States by Dutton Children's Books,
a division of Penguin Books USA Inc.
375 Hudson Street, New York, New York 10014

Designer: Barbara Powderly
Printed in Hong Kong by South China Printing Co.
First Edition　　10 9 8 7 6 5 4 3 2 1

**The art in this book is mixed-media collage, using watercolors,
pastels, ink, cut paper, and lamb's wool.**

LOURDES LIBRARY
GWYNEDD MERCY COLLEGE
GWYNEDD VALLEY, PA 19437

DISCARD